TYRA OF THE SHADOWS

First edition. April 21, 2024.

Copyright © 2024 Martha Wickham.

ISBN: 979-8227546869

Written by Martha Wickham.

Also by Martha Wickham

A Cursed Antique
Stories of a Cursed Antique
Found In Misty Falls: A Story of Magic
Beware of a Cursed Forest

Circle of Roses
Frankenstein's Bride: A Mystery
Circle Of Roses
The Haunted Rosebuds
Emily's Darkness
Tyra of the Shadows
Abigail's Road of Terror
The Rose Cases: Sylvie's Diary
The Roses: Voices in the Dark
The Roses: A Rose in the Forest
Mystery of Frankenstein's Bride Collection: Ghosts of the Circle

Summer Screams
Summer Night Screams: Unexplainable Horror Stories
Summer Night Screams: Mysterious Horror Tales

Summer Night Screams: Ghosts of Summer
Eternally Beautiful Summer Nights

Witch Lane
Nightmare in a Bottle

Standalone
Gardens and Dreams: Hearts Quest
Led By Obsession
Relaxed Poetry
Wishes, Gems, Disasters
Woodland Escape
Flames Of Fate
Terror Under The Tree: The Cursed Nutcracker
By Dawn: All the Dust and Lilies

Watch for more at https://readmarthawickham.com/.

Table of Contents

M A R T H A   W I C K H A M

TYRA OF THE SHADOWS

Paranormal
Child Of Frankenstein's Bride

Shadows danced all over Tyra's wall. The thirteen-year-old wondered why. Was it the spirits or a small breeze? She didn't feel a breeze. She liked to watch them and listen to the sounds of the old house. Her adoptive mother, Margaret, could be heard downstairs preparing dinner.

Her adoptive father, Frankie, could be heard calling to her. "Rain is coming!" Tyra rolled her eyes when she heard the thunder. He appeared in her doorway. "Don't worry. There won't be any leaks in this old house," he told her. They could hear a few raindrops start to come down. "I want you coming down for dinner," he said.

With a nod, she jumped up, straightened her black dress, and went down to dinner. The house was so big, but nothing fancy. It reminded Tyra of a large box, and she had lived there with them since she was about five. That was as far back as she could remember. The Smythes loved their old home. It was worth keeping.

. . . .

TYRA LAY IN BED AFTER a good night's sleep. The only sounds she heard were crickets and the storm. It was the perfect time for ghosts to haunt. She had searched for them before but never found them. Not last night either. The dancing flame was probably predicting the storm, and outside it was muddy.

The clicking of heels could be heard on the floor. Hattie, her babysitter, appeared in the doorway. Her blonde hair was pinned back, and her white lace dress was spotless. "I'm going to be staying here about four months," Hattie Cunningham said. Tyra sat up in surprise. "Your parents are going to London for a while, and I was asked to be your nanny."

Tyra shook and jumped out of bed in her wrinkled nightgown. Her babysitter was perfect, and her rules were also. Tyra hated them. "I want to see my mother!" she demanded. Her long black hair had grown all the way down her back.

Hattie got out of the way, afraid to argue with Tyra.

Tyra ran to Frankie, finding him in the living room. "No, I don't want you to go!"

"It's okay. We'll leave some money for you with Hattie, and I'll write. And I promise I'll bring you something back," he said reassuringly.

Tyra was thirteen but couldn't resist a gift from London. It would take a while to get there by boat. She hugged him. He had already packed. It wasn't long after she hugged both her parents that they left.

Hattie entered the house with two suitcases and went to her room, which was on the other side of the house from Tyra's.

Tyra didn't want to stay with Hattie. Her stare said how serious she was. Tyra did feel secure, though.

Hattie was a college student and was working part-time.

Frankie picked up his suitcases, and Margaret did also. "I promise I'll write to you as soon as I get there, Ty." He pinched her cheek and went on his way. He was very tall, and his suit seemed to make him even taller. Her mother hugged her and left as well.

Tyra sat by Hattie on the couch and asked, "Want to play cards?"

Hattie shook her head no. "Want lunch?"

Tyra agreed, and they went into the kitchen. They had leftovers, but the Italian food was so good. While the food was being warmed, Tyra went upstairs to put a dress on. Meanwhile, Hattie looked around the first floor. It was a mess, and it needed to be cleaned. She wanted to clean it immediately.

Out the window, large gray clouds from the night before seemed to be stalking them. By the time Tyra was eating, the rain poured, creating puddles outside. "Don't you go out in this," Hattie told Tyra.

Tyra shook her head no indicating she never would. She did have school the next day, so hopefully, it would be dry by then. If not, she would wear a long jacket and her big boots. All had started well.

During recess at school, Tyra sat by her friend Evelyn. "My parents have left for England, and Hattie is staying with me."

"No way," Evelyn replied.

"Yes, so we have to do something fun or interesting. My fourteenth birthday is coming soon. And just think, next fall, we will be in ninth grade. We should be in the same school. Also, I want to know who my real mother is."

Evelyn nodded in agreement.

"I'm thirteen now, and I don't remember the orphanage. When Hattie's not around, I'll search Margaret's room for my birth certificate or adoption papers. I've been thinking about it a lot lately," Tyra said.

"You've been growing a lot too. You're like five feet two now," Evelyn said with a giggle. "Let me know what you find."

Tyra nodded.

After school, Tyra got home and kicked off her shoes, then threw down her books. There was a note from Hattie that said, "Ty, I will be at a college class until five in the evening. At that time, I will fix you dinner. See ya." Tyra decided to go to her parents' bedroom and search for her adoption papers.

She sifted through Margaret's chest by the bed, then headed for Frankie's desk. No birth certificate, but she saw the name Tyra and grabbed that handful of papers. There it was. There was so much writing, and it kept saying "adopted." They were adoption papers. Just like Margaret said, she was adopted at three. Her mom's name was Terra Green, and Tyra's last name was Green. She was born in Chicago. Soon, Tyra could get a real copy of her birth certificate from the state, which should tell her who her father was. She would need it to get her first job anyway. It didn't say anything about her father, but it did state that although her mother was unmarried when Tyra was born, she was staying with someone named Jack. Who was he? Probably a boyfriend. Maybe even her father. How would she find him? It also said she was taken away by the state because Terra was unfit to be a mother. It stated more than a birth certificate did. Her mother didn't want her to go. Maybe she still wanted her or wanted to see her.

Tyra popped up with a flutter and nervously ran to her room with the papers. Hattie wouldn't know they were missing, so she kept them in her desk in her room. What a beautiful name, Terra Green. Tyra wondered if her face was beautiful as well. She was probably just like her mom, with long black hair and brown eyes. Tyra lay on her bed thinking of how she would meet her. Maybe Evelyn or Hattie would have some answers. How many Jack Clearsons were in Chicago in the 1930s? Not a lot of people knew her mother personally, but they knew who she was.

As Tyra lay there, she heard Hattie's green car pull up. She put the papers away and sat up. Hattie came in to ask how her day at school went, and Tyra said, "Same old stuff. How did yours go?"

"We watched a film and learned some Spanish." With a shrug of her shoulders, Hattie was off to start dinner.

Tyra just needed to get the white pages to look for a Jack Clearson, but they were in the kitchen cupboard. She went downstairs, where she could smell chicken and rice with sauce. She would grab the white pages when dinner was over.

Now it was time for homework. Hattie kept staring at her, so Tyra got up and said, "I'm going upstairs to do my homework. I'm having trouble in math."

Luckily for Tyra, Hattie brought a hot dinner plate with a drink up to her. Tyra was working on homework when she came in.

After eating, Tyra went downstairs and rinsed her plate in the sink. She got the telephone directory and started looking through the white pages. There he was, Jack Clearson, east of Chicago. There was only one. It couldn't have been easier—except he was east, and she was south. She wasn't going to ask Hattie to take her. Hattie would probably think there was trouble because she worried a lot.

Tyra could ask Evelyn to go with her by public transportation. It would be easier with a friend. Tyra tore out the page, circled his name, and took the page up to her room to be stuffed in her desk.

Tyra knew the address was a street near the shopping strips. There were many old houses there. She didn't want anyone to know yet, so she asked Evelyn if she wanted to hang out there after school so Tyra could watch and see if Jack would come out. She was even more in luck when Hattie handed her ten dollars, which was part of what her mother left for her.

The girls went after school, and Evelyn was laughing and smiling. Tyra bought them candy.

"Where did you get that money?" Evelyn asked.

"My parents left it for me before they went to England. I'm alone with my nanny, Hattie, remember?"

"What's she like?" Evelyn asked.

"Strict, but nice and quiet. She has a car," Tyra said.

"Wow, maybe she could drive us somewhere."

Tyra stared at the three-story house across the street and nodded.

"Why do you keep looking at that house?" Evelyn asked.

"I found out my mom's name, and the guy's name that lives there was on the adoption papers. It didn't say he was my father, but I think he was her boyfriend. I want to meet him," Tyra said. "My birth name was Green. Now it's Smythe."

Evelyn breathed with excitement. "Let's go over there. What's his name?"

"Jack Clearson."

"Sounds like a rich man." Evelyn grabbed Tyra by the hand, and they walked to the area right across his house on Silver Street. They could see a man inside.

He noticed them and came outside. Looking casual and clean-shaven, he was nothing like Frankie. "Is there anything you need? You girls okay?"

"We're fine," Tyra said. "To tell you the truth, I'm Tyra Smythe. My mom was Terra Green. I was adopted by the Smythes. Your name was on my adoption papers." Maybe this was easier than she thought. Good thing she had Evelyn with her.

Jack looked her up and down. She reminded him of Terra. "I heard about you. Terra was my girlfriend around 1933. Afterward, she got engaged to a banker named Nathaniel Johnston. They never married, I believe, because she got very sick with pneumonia. They had already taken her child—you—away when she was three, and I helped take care of her when she was dying. That was why they had me on the adoption papers."

"So you're not my father?" Tyra asked.

"No. Maybe it was Nathaniel. They had an on-again, off-again relationship about fourteen years ago," he said.

"Can you ask her?" Tyra asked.

"No. She died last year, Tyra."

Tyra looked pale. "She was young then."

"Come on inside. I can give you a picture of her and show you where she was staying."

They all headed inside. "This is my friend Evelyn. We go to the same school."

"Hello, Evelyn," Jack said.

"Hi," she replied.

They went inside the house and proceeded upstairs. Making a left, they came to the room that was Terra's. It was decorated in white and fuchsia. "These are the sheets she slept in. We haven't washed them," Jack said. They sat down on the bed, and he handed Tyra a headshot of Terra. Her mother did not smile for her picture. Her hair was halfway pinned up, and she wore a white lacy blouse.

"Thank you," Tyra said.

"I met your mother at her sixteenth birthday party. We got close, and she came here for dinner. After, we became friends."

She tried to feel her mother like she had a sixth sense but couldn't. "Can I ask you a question? Have you ever seen her ghost?"

"No, never. But I've met Dr. Frankenstein. He's known for his science experiments. He has brought the dead back to life. We were so grief-stricken when she died that he said he was going to bring her back to be Frankenstein's bride," Jack explained.

"When?" Tyra asked, starting to doubt him.

"Soon. She's still in the nearby cemetery if you want to go see her," Jack said.

"Of course. I want to know everything. Is my grandma alive? Where did my mother live?" Tyra asked.

"She's alive, but I don't know where she is. I can write down Terra's old address. She always lived there and was afraid of the ghosts. They were the reason she was glad to stay with me. She didn't want to die in her haunted house. Her mother came by every day."

"I'll look in the white pages and see if I can write to her. This is the best day! I want to go to the cemetery. I don't want my mother to be undead, though," Tyra said. "Let's go get lunch first, Evelyn. I'm buying." She picked up her mother's picture, and her hand shook.

They walked down the stairs. "Thank you so much for your help, Jack. I will never forget this."

"I'll take you guys out to lunch next week, okay?" Jack said.

Tyra hesitated and said, "That will be fine."

"Be by Sunshine Cafe at noon next weekend," he added with a smile and shut the door.

"Ty, are you sure we should come back to meet him for lunch? That sounded a little weird," Evelyn said.

"Yes, I'm so curious. If my mom will be the bride of Frankenstein, I'll want to know," replied Tyra. "Let's go. I'm starving." They walked to a small sandwich shop they were close to.

While scarfing down a tuna sandwich, Evelyn asked, "Where is the cemetery?"

"It's a few blocks down. We've all been down here before." When they finished their sandwiches, they began walking to the cemetery. Tyra assured her it wouldn't be far. She wished she'd had flowers for her mother.

It didn't take them long to find the Terra Belinda Green tombstone. "Maybe next weekend, you can come home with me. Hattie will come to pick me up in less than an hour. Do you want a ride home?"

"Yes."

"I'll ask if you can spend the night next weekend."

"Scared?" Evelyn asked, giggling.

"No. Okay, just a little." Tyra laughed too, and they spent some quiet time sitting on Terra's grave. "I'm not going to be alone if my mom's coming to get me from the grave."

"If I can't spend the night, you have Hattie," Evelyn said.

"She'll let you."

Chapter Two

"Hattie, me and Evelyn are going to get lunch at a nearby shop. Then we'll be back later in the afternoon, and she'll spend the night. We want to go for a walk on a trail down the road," Tyra said that warm afternoon.

"Okay, just be back before evening." Hattie's hair was pinned up in a messy bun. She was baking something with cinnamon that smelled good—cinnamon rolls!

Tyra smelled the rolls and ran up to her room to brush her hair.

Hattie entered. "Did you need more money? I can give you ten dollars more."

"Yes, Evelyn and I are walking a long way to a shop with chicken and sandwiches. That's why we'll be gone for a while. We may stop along the way. I want the money in case I see something I want to buy."

Hattie reentered with the money and placed it on Tyra's desk.

"Hattie?"

"Yes."

Tyra hesitated. "You know I was adopted?"

Hattie nodded.

"I read my adoption papers." She pulled the papers out of her desk.

Hattie looked them over.

"I found out my mother died young last year. Her name was Terra Green. We went to see her grave. That's why we were over by the cemetery. How did you know we were there?" asked Tyra.

"It wasn't far from where I dropped you off. How far does your friend live from here?" Hattie asked.

"About fifteen minutes. She walks far. We are close friends. We'll be in high school next year."

"You be careful walking. That trail can't go far. This is the city," Hattie offered.

"I know. We'll probably just eat, then look at some shops and maybe my mother's grave again."

There was an echoing knock at the door. "It's Evelyn." Tyra ran all the way downstairs after grabbing her money and opened the door. "We're going to eat lunch now! We need our energy to walk." She waved to Hattie from downstairs and shut the door behind her.

"Let's go. Jack Clearson is probably already there," Evelyn said. With that, they began walking quickly to the shop to have lunch.

As they walked, it got hotter. "I'm glad I didn't wear heels," Tyra said.

Just as Evelyn said, when they got there, Jack was waiting. They said hello, and Jack ordered lunch for the girls. Tyra was serious, and Evelyn looked like she was ready to laugh.

"I haven't heard anything about Terra becoming the bride of Frankenstein. I suppose she already is. She just needs to rise from the grave," Jack said with a grave tone. "What is it?" he asked.

"How would it feel if your mother was supposed to come back from the dead?" Tyra asked. "I mean it's cool I'm the bride of Frankenstein's daughter, but it's weird to think about. I keep waiting to find out I have powers."

"Maybe you do."

A man placed their food on the counter, and they took it.

"If we go see her grave, maybe she won't be in it," Tyra suggested.

"Honey, she is in her grave. You're right. Maybe it isn't a great idea to bring our loved ones back from the dead." Jack smiled, and they were given tall cold drinks. "You know what? There's a cool shop down the road with a lady who sells metaphysical things. We can go there before we go to the cemetery."

Both girls quickly agreed. After finishing large shredded chicken sandwiches, Jack led them to the shop. "Are you sure you're not my father?" Tyra asked him as they walked there.

"No. We'll find out once we find Nathaniel Johnston," Jack said.

"Do you have a car?" Tyra asked.

"Yes, but it's not working right now." He led the way to a small store that had shelves covered in blue velvet and smelled of burnt candles. The lady who worked there glanced up from her book.

Tyra lifted her eyes, and they began looking at interesting items.

"May I help you?" the lady asked. "We have many items. They are amazing. Some tell the future. Some conjure ghosts, and we have books on how to do it."

"We are just looking right now," Evelyn said.

Tyra touched the blue velvet table and shelf covers. "It's so soft."

"I can sell you one for your table." The lady in the flowy blue dress handed one to Tyra. There was a price tag, and it wasn't much.

There were also candles that weren't priced very much. "Affordable," Tyra said to the mysterious sales lady.

Her bracelets jingled. "We have other things that are affordable." She gestured to a table that had cheaper items. She managed to grab a cheap Ouija board.

"Don't talk to evil spirits," Jack said.

"We won't communicate with those," Tyra answered.

She didn't think Jack was her father. They didn't really look alike except for the dark hair. She was like her mother. She assumed he thought he wasn't. Besides, he had brought up Nathaniel Johnston. "Did you get any leads on Nathaniel Johnston?"

"No," he replied, shaking his head.

Tyra would look in the white pages if she had to. Walking over to Evelyn, she gripped the Ouija board and said, "Tonight. You are spending the night, remember?"

Evelyn nodded. "What's next?"

"Let's stop by my mom's grave. I want to see if they dug her up." Tyra did not want them to.

Tyra paid for her three items and stuffed them in Evelyn's large bag. "Here you go, Evy."

Heading for the door, Tyra said to Jack, "You coming?"

He shook his head no. "If the bride of Frankenstein is out walking around, I'll find out tonight."

Tyra didn't know what to think. The girls just went out the door and began walking toward the graveyard. When they arrived, it seemed everything was intact. No grave disturbance. There was just a small mound on it. She whacked herself in the head. "I didn't think to get flowers again! I don't like all this stuff. I wonder if Jack would say something to me if I called the police."

"Don't give him your address. I wonder if they can help you find your father," Evelyn said.

"They won't. Jack isn't any help. I'll just look myself. I'll think about going to the police. We don't have a phone. I don't like this."

When they got home, it felt much cooler in the house. They grabbed drinks and the telephone directory and went upstairs. Tyra did find a Nathaniel Johnston—she actually found two of them. "Evelyn, another big house to go look at later. I found Nathaniel."

"Good." Evelyn took everything out of her bag. They laid the blue velvet table cover, the candles, and the Ouija board in front of them on the floor.

"I'll go get a couple candlesticks. We will try a séance and use the board tonight," Tyra said.

"Hattie, where are the candlesticks?" Tyra called.

"In the hallway by the kitchen!" Hattie answered.

She and Evelyn raced there and grabbed two.

Hattie appeared. "Be careful with those. Matches are in the kitchen."

"Thanks," Tyra responded. "Have you ever seen a ghost in here?"

"No, never," Hattie responded.

"Hopefully, we will," Tyra said as she headed for the kitchen. She grabbed the matches.

"We won't light them now, not until tonight," she told Evelyn.

"My mom is coming by in the morning to come and get me," Evelyn said.

Tyra nodded. "We're going to try a séance. I read about them in the paper."

"I don't want you to do that. I told you I haven't seen any ghosts here. When the wind blows, you can hear it loud. This is an old house. Your dad said it was built in the 1790s," Hattie said.

"We'll just try. It probably won't work." Tyra went to her room as Evelyn followed.

"Is it even worth the time?" Evelyn asked.

"No, but this is." Tyra pulled out a rolled-up Ouija board that looked like a map. She took the planchette out of Evelyn's purse. "I didn't tell Hattie we had this." They sat on the floor and felt the beautiful soft velvet.

"What do you think about what Jack said? About your mom coming back as the bride of Frankenstein?" Evelyn asked.

"I don't think it will work, but I don't want them to dig her up. I won't tell Hattie because I don't want her to know. I don't think she will approve." Tyra laid the Ouija board on the velvet. "It doesn't have to be nighttime for us to do this." She got up to close the curtains in her small room and shut the door. They could hear Hattie downstairs in the kitchen.

"Is she a student?" Evelyn asked.

"Yes, Hattie has long blond hair that she pins up when she studies. Sometimes she wears makeup, but I don't think she's into it that much. A lot of people aren't anymore. Should we cut our hair? Not short, just shoulder's length." They both had hair all the way down their backs.

"Okay, but I have to ask my mom first."

"I wish we had a phone. Margaret said we will get one. We need one. I can't wait."

They grabbed their hair just to look at it. "My hair is so thick." Tyra's hair was coarse and black. Evelyn's was brown and unhealthy. The Ouija was by them.

Tyra positioned her hands on the planchette, and Evelyn did as well. "Hello, is anyone here?" Tyra asked.

The plank moved to "yes," but very slowly.

"Wow," Evelyn said, shaking.

"Is this the spirit of my mother?" Tyra giggled.

It moved to "no."

"Are you from our attic?"

It moved to "yes."

"Well, where are you from originally?"

"The field," it responded.

Thunder sounded. Another spring storm was coming. "It's gonna rain. Late tonight, you will hear the sounds if it does," she told Evelyn.

"Who are you?" Tyra asked.

"Abby," it responded.

"Are you alone?" She didn't like the thought of ghosts moving in.

The board responded with a "yes."

Tyra breathed a sigh of relief. "Is there anything important I must know?"

The planchette moved quickly to spell "bride of Frankenstein."

"My mother? She's coming back?"

It moved to "yes" and spelled "soon," followed by "don't trust Jack."

Both girls heard a moan, and they heard Hattie running up the steps. The girls gave a goodbye, and the board responded as well. Tyra quickly threw the board under the bed, and they left the velvet. The candles were not lit.

Hattie stormed in. "I heard that! You girls are messing with spirits."

"We were just trying to do a séance when we heard something."

Tyra's excuse wasn't working because, just then, Hattie picked up the planchette, which was lying by the bed.

"Tyra, do you have a Ouija board in here?" Hattie asked.

"Yes, I grabbed it with the velvet covering," Tyra responded.

Hattie looked under the bed and took the Ouija board. "There will be no boards tonight. There is a storm coming." She went back downstairs and put the board in the dresser of the room she was staying in across from Margaret and Frankie's room. The girls did not have it now, and Hattie tossed the worry out of her head and went to get started on pasta.

Out of boredom, the girls found books to read, listened to the thunder, and planned how short they were going to cut their hair. There were so many sounds, and the wind was strong. But Tyra was sure some of the footsteps weren't Hattie's—they were Abby's.

"You don't suppose that's . . . ?" Evelyn asked.

"Yes, I know that's the ghost. We'll look for her tonight. I like her, but I don't want to go in that attic," Tyra said.

"Abby?" Evelyn asked.

"Yes."

They picked everything up off the floor and put them away in a chest with drawers.

"When my birthday comes up, will you come?" Tyra asked.

"Of course," Evelyn responded.

"You can help me plan it tonight. We'll just come up with ideas. But first, the dance is coming. Do you have a dress?"

"Yes, Ty. My mom said I could wear my older sister's dress. It's dark blue with beads. It doesn't fit her anymore. I can't wait. Do you have one?"

"No, I have to get one," Tyra responded. Then she took a paper pad and pen out of her desk.

As they wrote down ideas, the dark curtains began to move. "Maybe it's a draft," Evelyn suggested.

"No, I think it's the ghost. They're still moving." The curtains moved gently, and Tyra pulled them open like a detective. The sky showed that night had just fallen, and it was starting to rain.

The bedroom door opened, and they heard footsteps. "I think she wants us to follow her." They both looked at each other and followed the small sounds out the door. It sounded like creaking floorboards. In the hallway, they could see a light coming from upstairs. They stepped forward to investigate.

Going up the steps, they saw nothing. The light from the moon showed through a window, and the space wasn't big. The door to the attic was open a little, and it opened more. A glowing light that didn't seem like moonlight came from the attic.

"She wants us to go to the attic—exactly where we didn't want to go," Evelyn said.

They both went in. At the sight of nothing but dust, Evelyn sat down.

Tyra went to check out a chest. When she opened it, there were all these items that belonged to a girl. "These could be Abby's." She dug to the bottom.

"Maybe she just wants to be friends," Evelyn said.

Tyra nodded in agreement. The clothing—nightshirts and a blouse—was in good shape. Quickly, she grabbed something soft and pulled it out. She stood and held it up. It was a dress! It was dark blue with black lace trim. "A dress!" She held it up to herself. "I need one for the dance."

She tried it on over her clothes. The dark blue was still shiny, and the lace made it seem more grown-up and formal. Tyra loved the color. It was perfect. Now she wouldn't have to ask Evelyn if she could borrow a dress. "Do you like it?"

"Yes, it's amazing! But how will you clean it? Won't the ghost mind?" her friend asked.

"I'll have to ask Hattie to have it cleaned. She can use the money my parents left me. The ghost may mind, but I'll wear it only one night."

They ran downstairs to Hattie.

"What if that's why we were led to the attic?" Evelyn asked.

"Probably."

They heard a ghostly moan.

"What was that?" Hattie asked.

"We found a dress in the attic. Can you have it cleaned?" Tyra asked.

"Yes."

Just then, they watched as shadows from the candles danced on the wall. They kept watching as they became people. Hattie's eyes widened as the people ran away, and there were no more shadows. "That's strange," she said.

"Yes," Tyra replied.

For the rest of the night, none of them once went in the direction where the shadow people went.

"That was the creepiest thing I have ever seen," Evelyn said.

Quickly, Hattie ran to her room on the left side of the house, where the shadow people went. She grabbed all her belongings and left the room. The door behind her rattled.

They walked up to the second story, and Hattie chose a new room. Both girls did not know if they should be glad she was so close now. When all three sat down in Tyra's room, they were glad. "We met a ghost named Abby on the Ouija board. We think this used to be her house," Tyra said.

"That dress is a little old-fashioned, but I can use the money your parents left to have it cleaned," Hattie said.

• • • •

AS TYRA WAS AT THE dance, Hattie decided to have a little gathering of her own and had some friends over. The music played loudly as they danced and ate hors d'oeuvres. Candles were lit, and a chandelier hung over the dinner table.

As they sat and ate, a guest in a suit asked, "Hattie, what are you going to college for?" The man sipped his wine.

"I want to teach small children. It will be a while before I'm ready, but I am a nanny here to one teenage girl." Hattie stood. "I must get dinner." She served them a juicy pot roast, potatoes, and vegetables.

After eating, people wandered away from the table. It was an impressive party, and two ladies wandered upstairs to check out the house. Everyone went in different directions.

As Hattie was finishing her meal, she heard a scream come from the left side of the house. She ran to Margaret and Frankie's bedroom. There was a couple in there, and the frightened lady had her mouth wide open. A shadow ran across the wall, and a large bookcase fell on top of Hattie. The woman screamed again. When her boyfriend lifted the bookcase, Hattie lay there with broken glass around her, and her arm was cut. The blood dripped onto her white dress.

The party was over. As people were going out the door, Tyra came in. "Hattie!" she called as she ran to her.

"The shadow people cut me." That was what they were called from then on. "After dinner, I heard a scream, so I had to come in here. There was a large shadow moving across the wall, and the bookcase fell on me."

"Are you okay?" Tyra asked as she grabbed bandages and something to clean the Hattie's wound with.

"I think so. My arm hurts. After you dress it, I want to take painkillers and go to bed. Let's try not to come in here. In the morning, we can clean the glass off the floor," Hattie said with disheveled hair.

Tyra nodded.

"Can you fix yourself a plate in the kitchen?" Hattie asked.

Tyra nodded again as she taped the bandage in place. Entering the kitchen, she could see the rainbows from the chandelier dancing around the table. She blew out all the candles as Hattie went to bed with her medicine.

Before going to her room, Tyra looked in on Hattie as she slept. The night was still, and she turned off all the lights except a small one in the bathroom.

Chapter Three

Come morning, Hattie Cunningham entered Tyra's room, dressing on her arm. "How was the dance?" she asked.

"Good. I danced with a boy. I think he wants to be my boyfriend. He asked me where I lived and if he could walk me home sometime. I said yes," Tyra responded quickly.

"That's great. Have you been speaking to that ghost?" Hattie asked.

"No."

"It hasn't threatened you or made any strange sounds for wearing that dress?" Hattie asked.

"No. I think she wanted me to," Tyra answered.

"Tyra Smythe, please don't ever do that again." Hattie shook her head.

"I'm going to return that dress to the trunk upstairs," Tyra said.

"Okay, that's a good idea. Come down to breakfast as soon as you're ready."

Tyra nodded, and Hattie was off. Tyra smoothed her hair and put on a dress. Grabbing the dress from the closet, she headed toward the attic. Opening the attic door, she saw nothing but dust. She opened the chest and placed the dress inside. A breeze pushed it closed. Tyra looked around. She felt the breeze and didn't want to stay. Before she left the attic, she thanked Abby for letting her wear the dress, although she was unsure whether Abby really did want her to.

For a few seconds, it was quiet. Then she heard a few footsteps. Tyra left the attic quickly, unsure.

"Do you think the shadows on the wall you saw last night were ghosts?" Tyra asked.

"Yes, they are shadow people," Hattie answered, looking up from her notebook she was studying.

"Is college hard?" Tyra asked.

"Yes, you have to do all your homework to get good grades. What about you? Do you have any homework?" Hattie asked.

"Yes. But did you know I am looking for my biological father?" asked Tyra.

"Yes. Let's get your birth certificate to make it easy."

"That will take a while, but okay. I still want to find this Nathaniel Johnston my mom was engaged to."

"Get the address. We can drive by, then stop by the records office and ask them to order the birth certificate," Hattie said. She sat up to brush her hair and get her purse.

Tyra ran up to get her shoes and the page with Nathaniel's name and address. They left the house immediately. Tyra said, "My mother used to live a few blocks from Nathaniel."

They got to the other side of town. "There it is," Tyra said, pointing. They stopped across the street from the large home. There were cars parked in front of the house. The houses in the neighborhood behind it were so large that Tyra couldn't see far beyond it.

"I don't know what to do," Tyra said.

"Don't do anything. We'll get the certificate in about a couple weeks and know if he even has the same name."

Tyra nodded, and they were off for the certificate to be ordered and to get some lunch. "You can pay for the certificate with the money my mom left me," Tyra said.

Hattie nodded. "I have news. You got a letter from your father yesterday. He must have written to you right away. I got one as well with some money to have a phone installed." She smiled. "They must miss you. Don't talk to your father until you ask Frankie, okay?"

"Okay," Tyra said, taking a deep breath, then sipping some juice.

When they got home, Hattie went to the attic, locked the door from the outside, put the key in her pocket, then made plans to have a phone installed that week.

Tyra sat at her wooden desk, working on her math homework. She was good at the pre-algebra they were teaching and was almost done. She closed her curtains because night had fallen. Then she went back to her homework. A sudden thud sounded from above. It was the attic! Tyra did not like staying beneath the attic now that there were ghosts. Footsteps began, and Tyra called, "Hattie?"

There was no response, and Tyra assumed Hattie had fallen asleep. Quickly, Tyra completed the last few math problems and went to the attic, one staircase up. Trying the door, she saw it was locked. On the second floor, Hattie's door was shut. Tyra went downstairs and turned off all the lights and checked that the doors were locked. She didn't see any shadow people. There wouldn't be any shadows if there weren't any lights. When thuds kept sounding from the attic, Tyra took a candle upstairs to the attic door and called, "Abby?"

There was a moan.

"Abby, can you keep it down? Are you angry the attic door is locked?" Tyra asked.

Thud.

"Are the shadow people evil?"

Thud.

"Is there a way to get rid of them? Are they trapped downstairs?" Tyra listened through the door, wishing Evelyn was around.

Thud.

"Did you used to live here?"

A moan was heard, and next was a quiet "yes."

"What was that?" Hattie asked, standing behind Tyra.

"I was communicating with the ghost," Tyra answered.

"I locked the door. Stay away from there," Hattie replied.

"She said the shadow people are evil and they are downstairs."

"I can't do anything tonight, just stay up here mostly and get to bed. My mother is stopping by in the morning."

Tyra nodded.

• • • •

WHEN TYRA WOKE, SHE could hear talking downstairs. It was Hattie talking to her mother. Tyra went to the top of the stairs and watched them in the kitchen. "This house is haunted now by evil shadows." She showed her bandaged arm to her mother. "I'm afraid to leave to even go to school."

Her mother nodded. Her large thick dress was like a robe, and her hair was in a messy bun. "I miss you, my Hattie." The lines on her eyes said it was true.

"I want to quit, but I can't. Her parents aren't here. They wrote and sent money to have a phone installed so that we can talk. Gosh, they're all the way in England! But I can't wait to get a new phone. I can call them whenever I need them and you or anyone else." She hugged her mother. "I'll have it done right away!"

"Can I bring you something, Hat?" her mother asked.

"Just food, a few dresses, and paper for school. You know, I took the kids' Ouija board and hid it in the room, which is now the haunted heart of the house—that and the attic."

"Show me the room," her mother said.

They walked twenty steps to the left of the kitchen. When Hattie opened the door, the room was a mess. There were no ghosts. "Watching kids is hard, dear. Do you still want to teach them?" her mother asked.

"Yes."

"I am getting a phone today too so you can call me. Call anytime, Hattie, especially if you're scared or it's an emergency," her mother said.

Hattie nodded. "I will. I was staying in that room and moved to the second floor." The house creaked as they walked.

"I am not sure when I'm coming back with your things. Maybe tomorrow," her mother said and kissed her on the forehead. They headed for the door.

"Thanks, Mom," Hattie said.

Her mother stepped in the doorway to leave. As she looked up, she saw Tyra on the top of the stairs in her nightgown.

"Mom, that's Tyra," Hattie said.

Her mom went to Tyra. "Hello, dear. I'm Hattie's mom, Isabelle."

"Hi," Tyra responded.

"Is there anything I can bring for her?" Isabelle asked Hattie.

"I don't know. Anything a young teen would like," Hattie said, and Tyra nodded.

"Wait, Mom," she said, then ran to the closed haunted room she stashed the Ouija board in. After digging through junk, she found it and gave it to her mother. "Can you toss it out?"

"Of course," she said and left.

"It's better off gone. They probably wanted you to use it," Hattie explained.

"All right, I guess I don't need it then," Tyra said.

"You shouldn't talk to those things at all. There's a problem here. I'm going into town to ask them to come here and have a phone installed. It's what your mother wants. It's best, Tyra. She doesn't know what's happened. Did I give you your father's letter?"

"No, I found it in the kitchen and read it. He seemed happy, but worried," Tyra said.

"Okay, good." Hattie jumped and ran to the stairs. "I'm going upstairs to get dressed and ask them to come put in a phone. I can't wait. Want to come?"

Tyra jumped up as well. "Yes, the Smythes are getting a phone!"

They held hands as they walked up the stairs. Tyra forgave Hattie for getting rid of the Ouija board. It was a relief for the both of them. Tyra secretly hoped her parents would not be there for her birthday party, but maybe they would be.

Neither of them could wait for the phone, so three hours later, a black rotary phone was installed.

Hattie called Margaret and Frankie almost immediately, telling them the house was haunted. Hattie was told to call a priest and have him bless the house, and she made an appointment to have him come the next day when Tyra was in school.

Little did they know Jack Clearson was snooping around outside. All Tyra saw from the second-story window was a man in black walking around the property. There were about five other large houses, and she and Hattie did not know any of those people. Tyra heard whispers that sounded like young men, and there was a shadow moving down to the front door. Jack could not be seen, but he let out a loud yell.

Running to a front window, Tyra could see blood on his hand, and a large piece of wood had swung down from above the door and hit him hard. It must have been the shadow people scaring him off. Tyra felt safe but wondered if her mother had returned as the bride of Frankenstein yet.

Tyra went to the front door, and the wood was hanging down by a nail on the left side of the door. What was Jack doing there? She couldn't be related to such a man. She needed to find Nathaniel Johnston to see if he was her father. That night, she would call him after Hattie headed to bed. But first, Hattie needed to know everything that had just happened.

Chapter Four

Before Evelyn and Tyra headed out to school, Tyra showed her the new phone and took down Evelyn's phone number. They walked up to the second floor and stuck their heads into Hattie's room.

Tyra said, "Bye, Hattie. I'm going to school."

"Wait! Your father said he was thinking about coming home early," Hattie said.

Tyra sighed.

"He's worried about the ghosts. He also wants someone to come fix the piece of wood hanging from the door. If you want to meet your father, you can." Hattie approached Tyra.

"I called Nathaniel Johnston last night, and he said he may be my father. He was engaged to my mother, Terra, and she told him she was pregnant," Tyra said.

"Really? What's the doubt?" Hattie asked.

"He thought she was dating other guys, but probably not. That's why they got engaged! He wanted me," Tyra said loudly.

"Wow, did he say anything about meeting you?" Hattie asked.

"No. I'll call him again," Tyra said.

"I wish he could come here, but the ghosts. I'll think about it. I want you to talk to your father Frankie. Maybe this afternoon or tomorrow," Hattie said.

Tyra nodded.

"Now go on to school, the both of you." Hattie waved both girls off.

As planned, while the girls were off at school, the priest came wearing black and a cross necklace that he kissed for protection. "Show me the worst areas of the house." He clutched a small Bible in his pocket. Hattie took him to the room she was staying in and opened the door. It was still a mess.

"They are shadows. They did this to me." She took off her bandage to reveal a long scab.

A bad feeling came over him, and he looked around. He even went into the walk-in closet. There was not a single sound. Then they heard it—a few steps on the second floor. The priest ran to the second floor.

Hattie went into Tyra's room. "Tyra says the footsteps are above her room almost every night. They come from the attic. She believes Abby the ghost used to live here, and Tyra found an old dress in the attic and wore it."

"Let's go." The priest was ready. He began flinging holy water around the room and prayed the house would be blessed.

Hattie went to the attic stairs, and they ascended them. They could hear furniture moving on the other side of the door. Hattie lifted her key to open it, and they saw dusty old furniture moving to other parts of room. It stopped when the priest entered. They searched everywhere, looked through the old chest, and even tried talking to the ghost. But all they got were footsteps. More prayers were said.

"Can I call you if I need you?" Hattie asked.

"Yes," the priest said at the doorway, and he pushed the large hanging board out of the way and examined it. "Call me in a week or so and let me know how the house is."

Hattie nodded and went inside to straighten up the room they were in on the left side of the kitchen. When she was done, the room looked better. She thought cleaning would help get rid of the ghosts in there. But when she left, she still shut the door behind her without locking it and felt better.

Shortly after Hattie sat down, there was a knock at the door. When she answered it, a man in white overalls stood there with a toolbox.

"I'm here to fix the hanging wood. I'm from the Fix It All company," he said.

Hattie pointed to the hanging wood. An easy job, just hanging from a nail. "There are others. It's strange." She didn't want to tell the man that the house was haunted and the shadow people did it. She stood in front of the doorway so he couldn't see inside the house. As she did, a glass of milk slid across the counter. She came outside and shut the door. They began walking around the house.

"This is where other boards fell down." Hattie pointed to a few hanging from the back of the white house.

"Yes, it looks like a prank. Either that, or this house is really old," the Fix It All man said.

"It is old." Hattie stood in front of the window, and a shadow person with no legs moved across the wall in their direction.

"What do you want done?" he asked. "Those are pretty high, but I can use a ladder."

"It would look better if you just nailed them back. I don't want Margaret telling me there are empty wood siding spots," she said, looking for the shadow ghost.

"Okay." He went to grab his ladder. Some of those spots were high, near the floor of the second floor.

As Hattie sat inside the house, she heard the man yell, then a crash. She looked out the window to see he had fallen off the top of the tall ladder and hit the ground. He was unconscious. She ran to the new phone to call local emergency services. After they said they were coming, she ran outside to the man.

He began opening his eyes but closed them again. In minutes, the emergency hospital vehicle arrived, and the emergency personnel put the man in the big white truck.

When the Fix It All man was gone, Hattie picked up his ladder and tools and put them in the back of his truck. The truck was parked right by the house, and Tyra would see it for sure when she came home in a couple of hours. It could be explained, but in her heart, Hattie blamed the shadow people. Now she knew they were bad.

She marched in the house right past the hanging wood at the door and yelled, "I know you're there! Come out, you cowards! You have to leave!" Just then, footsteps could be heard above in the attic, and Hattie ran to it with her keys.

"Abby!" she called out in the attic. It was deathly silent, and Hattie was curious about the chest and desk. She walked to the desk, pulled off the dirty sheet, sneezed at the dust and dirt, and sat down. Upon opening the desk, she saw dried-up old-fashioned pens, blank paper, and, in the back, a handful of letters. Bingo! They were from a girl named Abigail and sent to the address Hattie was at working as a nanny. They looked like they were from the late eighteen hundreds and written to Abigail's mother.

When Hattie opened a letter and read it quickly, she saw that Abigail, who was eleven, had written a few letters to her mother from camp. The first letter—whose paper was yellow and had an old dead-wood, earthy smell—was quite general. It said she liked the camp, there were a lot of kids, and she missed her mother. Abby was doing all the fun things kids did in camp: exploring, roasting around fires, and telling scary stories at night.

In the next letter, she began talking about all the scary stories and one of her favorites about a haunted area around that camp she hoped wasn't true. Some kids she talked to believed it, and some didn't. Hattie wondered what could have happened to Abigail, so she read on. Deep in thought, Hattie jumped when she heard the phone ring. She grabbed all the letters, stuffed them in her pocket, and ran downstairs to get the phone.

It was her mother. After the incident that day, she didn't tell her mother. She didn't want her to come by. Of course, her mother asked, "How are you?"

"I'm fine," she answered. "A priest came by today, but I still saw a ghost. One of them used to live here. I found letters from her in the attic. None of this happened before Tyra and Evelyn used the Ouija board. Did you get rid of it like I asked you to?"

"Yes, I did. I threw it out. I'll be over tomorrow, okay, dear?" her mom said.

"Okay. Things need to get back to normal here, and I have to go to school in a couple days. I'll call Margaret and Frankie and tell them how it's going. The priest wanted me to give him a report and tell him about the ghosts in a week. I don't know what we're going to do. Abigail's letters ought to be interesting."

When the phone call was over, Hattie went upstairs to her room and shut the door. She put the letters in the bottom drawer of her dresser and lay down on the bed. It was a small room with off-white ruffled curtains and an off-white bedspread. She thought about what she would say to Tyra about the truck parked outside. The truth: the man came to fix the wood panels and got nowhere because he fell. Fear swirled in her stomach because she did not want Frankie and Margaret to come home from their trip early.

She heard the front door—Tyra! Hattie forgot to lock the attic door. She got up to greet her.

"How was school?" she asked.

"It was fine, the same." Tyra looked slowly out the window at the truck.

"A man came to fix the house. He fell, Tyra, and he couldn't fix it. I had to call the hospital. I think I'll nail that piece of wood by the door myself. The ones that are higher up will have to hang."

Hang they did. As the spring rain came that night, the wind rustled everything and caused the hanging wood to swing back and forth. That night, that was all that could be heard. As Tyra did her homework, Hattie lay in bed, reading Abigail's letters.

Chapter Five

"Okay, I can't wait." Tyra hung up the phone.

"What did they say?" Hattie asked.

"They are getting on a boat to come home in a few days. It will take them a week to get here," Tyra responded.

"I knew it. What did you tell them?" Hattie asked.

"That I met Jack Clearson, but he wasn't my father. I told her the house is haunted because I used a Ouija board. She sounded worried and said she wanted to come home and throw me a birthday party. And the house is haunted," Tyra said and sat next to Hattie.

"They haunted my dinner party. I don't think they like parties. Is there anything we can do to get ready for them?" Hattie asked.

"If you drive me to the psychic shop I got the Ouija board from, maybe they have one," Tyra said.

"Have what?" Hattie asked.

"A spirit ball. How much money is left in the money Mom left me?" Tyra asked.

"About 110 dollars. But let's not spend it all since she's coming back early," Hattie said slowly.

"Okay, but we have enough money to get you one and me one as well. Then we could have lunch. And I should probably get a dress for my birthday party. I'll call Mom and ask her if we could spend it."

Tyra went to quickly call her mother and ask if she could spend the money at the hotel she was at. Before hanging up, she said, "Thank you, Mom. Bye." She turned to Hattie. "Here's what we'll do: we'll get a spirit ball and lunch, and then I'll save the rest toward a dress."

Hattie nodded.

Missing school that day, they went to buy spirit balls. Two was best for a large house. They got lunch, but no dress. There was not quite enough money. When they got home, they hung the spirit balls in their bedroom closets by ribbons and anticipated what would happen that night with the ghosts. Tyra's birthday wasn't for another month, so they had time.

"I'm inviting Evelyn and some boys and girls from school," Tyra told Hattie. "I think Nathaniel really is my father. Will you tell Margaret for me?" she asked.

"Yes," Hattie responded.

"I wanted to plan my party with Evelyn. I hope my mom lets me use the ideas." Tyra took a deep nervous breath.

"What?" Hattie asked.

"My mom is supposed to be the bride of Frankenstein. I think Jack dug her up so Dr. Frankenstein could bring her back," Tyra responded.

"Okay. You stay here, and I'll drive by the cemetery to check if she's there," Hattie said.

"Will you also see what's happening at Nathaniel Johnston's house?" asked Tyra.

"Okay. I'll be gone about an hour. Don't answer the door if someone comes," Hattie instructed.

Tyra nodded in agreement.

Hattie approached Nathan's house, which looked desolate. His car was gone, and it seemed no one else was around. He had a few newspapers and a delivered package at his door. She went out of her car and walked to the door. The package was labeled and unopened. Hattie knocked a few times on the door, but no one answered. It appeared he would be gone for a while.

She went to his mailbox, and just as she had suspected, it was full of mail—most of it addressed to Nathan Johnston. She slammed the metal door of the mailbox. He had been gone a little while. Hattie took the package and left it in his backyard so it would not get stolen.

Her gut told her something could be wrong. She had, at first, wanted to get the po'boy sandwiches but wasn't sure if she could eat them now. Quickly and suspiciously, she drove to the graveyard to check on Terra. She parked by the cemetery curb when she saw the grave was completely dug up. Not only that, but the whole coffin was also gone. Was it Tyra's bad luck? Was she destined to lose both parents? It was so gloomy. Quickly, Hattie drove to the police station.

While at the station, she explained the situation with Nathan and Terra's missing body. She also mentioned Jack, along with Dr. Frankenstein.

"We'll go to Nathan's house." The officer stood up.

"No one's there. I just went and knocked," Hattie said.

"We need to find out if he's missing," the officer said.

"I'll have Tyra try to keep calling," Hattie said.

"Okay, we'll be keeping an eye on the house."

"What about Terra's body?" Hattie asked.

"We'll get it back." The officer was sure.

"Please keep me updated," Hattie said.

"Yes, ma'am." The officer left the room.

· · · ·

AS THE DAYS WENT BY, Tyra kept trying to call Nathan, but there was no answer. The police didn't call, and Hattie thought they knew something.

The answer finally came when she got the newspaper. There was a small article on the front page with the headline nathaniel johnston killed in car accident. As Hattie read the story, she found that he was actually missing until they found his car smashed by the side of a road out in the forest. He didn't hit a tree—he was hit by someone. Since they didn't have his body, there was an investigation. Maybe he was injured, managed to crawl off, and died somewhere in the forest. No one knew, and Hattie wanted answers.

She explained this to Tyra, knowing she would want answers and maybe try to find them herself.

"They think my real dad is dead?" Tyra asked.

Hattie nodded.

Tyra sat down. She never met her real father, but Margaret and Frankie were good parents to her. She would stay where she was. Slowly, she said, "Can we go to the accident scene?"

"Yes, as long as there are no investigators there at the time. I'll drive you there, and it will be a nice ride into the woods," Hattie answered.

"Can we go tonight?" Tyra asked.

"It's better if we go this afternoon. The drive is not short, and we will be able to see better," Hattie said. "Do you think he's alive?"

"No, but I would like to see the accident scene," Tyra answered. She ran upstairs to get ready to go.

Hattie shuffled, hoping Tyra wouldn't tell her mother she took Tyra to an accident scene. Margaret was on her way home soon.

• • • •

THE RIDE DID NOT TAKE two hours, and no one was in sight. Hattie recognized the area because of a picture of where the mountains started.

Wearing boots, Tyra got out of the car and began to look around. "Dad!" she called.

Nathaniel was a very nice man, usually dressed in a suit and tie. He was a banker and desperately wanted to marry Terra—not just because of a baby. He was caring and gave to charities like a generous human being. There was no question he did not deserve this.

The girls walked through the area and started for the woods. "This is stupid," Tyra said. When they were ready to give up, she shouted, "Look!" She pointed at what was a long pile of dirt by the road. As they ran closer to it, it looked more like a grave mound.

"Let's call the police," Hattie said.

"I have to see." Tyra began digging with her hands through the top dirt, then used her nails to get through the earth. Nothing in the woods stirred. Twelve inches down, she hit clothing. It was a blue plaid shirt. Thinking it was a big body, Tyra pulled at the shirt hard. When she fell back, she choked down air. She dropped an arm in the dirt. It was just an arm. When she dug with both hands, she found a foot in a shoe, then the other arm. When she came to hair, she stopped. "What was going on here?"

"In the article, it said he liked to chop wood and sell some for a little extra cash. He also kept it for himself. They found an axe nearby, but I don't think he's done this to himself. He must have driven up here to chop wood and was killed. Maybe they crashed into his car on purpose." Hattie took a deep breath.

"Either way, we're going to the cops. They couldn't find this?" Tyra asked, annoyed.

"Maybe they weren't looking in this direction," Hattie said. "They need dogs. Let's get out of here now!" she demanded, grabbing Tyra's hand. They ran to the car and left.

The first place they stopped at was the same police station. "This is not how I want to remember my real father," Tyra said.

"And your real mother's the bride of Frankenstein," Hattie said. "Did they ever find her body?" she asked the police.

"Yes. But we haven't gotten it back. I don't know what they're doing in that science lab." The officer shook his head. "We'll go recover Nathaniel's dead body and notify his family. I'll let them know you found it."

"Okay, thanks," Tyra said, shaking a little. "Can we go home?" she asked Hattie.

"Yes, somewhere among all this, I need to find time to study. What will we tell your mother?" Both girls left the station.

On the way home, they felt both relieved and disturbed. Nathaniel was found, but the crime wasn't solved. That night, Hattie could hear Tyra crying, depressed about her life. At that moment, loud footsteps were heard in the attic.

"Can't you shut up?" Hattie shouted at Abby's ghost. "There are people mourning here! Have some respect!" Her bedroom door flew open, followed by her dresser drawers. The ghost was mad. Abby's letters went flying up in the air.

Tyra stopped crying and went to the door. "What happened?" she asked from her bedroom with her face red.

"Some psycho ghost got crazy. It will be okay." Hattie began picking up the letters.

"What are those?" Tyra asked.

"Letters," Hattie replied as she collected the rest of them. Now was not a good time to lie.

Tyra approached and looked at the envelope. It was from an Abigail. "Are these from Abby? And you didn't tell me." She quickly took one and read it.

Hattie was hoping Tyra would not become depressed. It was okay she knew about the letters, but it wasn't okay that Hattie was hiding them.

"She was at camp. I wonder if she died there. We may never know. They were sent to here. It sounds like she was happy." Tyra sniffed. "That's the way you want to be before you die. Poor Abigail . . . I wonder if she's buried in the same cemetery as my mother. Can I read these?" Tyra asked.

"Yes, I'm done with them. But I'm not sure the ghost doesn't mind us reading them. Be careful, okay?" Hattie said.

"I will." Tyra took the letters and went to her room. There were eight of them, and some were very long.

It seemed Tyra would be feeling better soon when Hattie came to her door.

"The police called. The officer said the family is grateful you found him, and they think you are his daughter. They said the family wants you to go to the funeral. He is being cremated and buried in the same cemetery as your mother." Hattie had given nice news.

"Good." Tyra tried to smile. "These letters are pretty good. I would like to go to the funeral and say goodbye to my real father."

"Great, it will be next weekend. I'll go with you. Would you like some lunch?" Hattie asked.

"Yes," Tyra said, unsure.

"I'll try to make us po'boy sandwiches," Hattie said.

As they nibbled on their sandwiches, Hattie worked on some homework. She had never made a po'boy before but did a pretty good job of it.

• • • •

THE FUNERAL WAS DAYS away from Margaret and Frankie coming home. Tyra and Hattie both dressed in black. When they got to the church, Tyra was very quiet because she didn't know anybody. She learned very little about Nathaniel during the speech by the pastor but did figure out who his sister and parents were. He had already been cremated and was ready to be put in the ground.

When they went outside, Hattie put fresh yellow roses on his grave. The funeral was over, and people began leaving. The old people she thought were her grandparents started leaving. Tyra wanted to introduce herself to her grandparents but wasn't sure it was them, so she kept quiet.

As Hattie walked around the cemetery, Tyra went back into the church. The stained glass windows were colorful, and she sat at a bench and prayed, praying that more bad things wouldn't happen. At that moment, she was glad Margaret was coming home. She said amen and went to get Hattie. "I can't wait for Mom to get home."

"It won't be long now," Hattie said while driving her forest-green car.

Chapter Six

When Frankie and Margaret got home, Tyra was so happy she clapped, hugged them, and grinned. When they found out their bedroom was the second haunted heart of the house, they moved out all their things to a large room on the second floor. Afterward, the room was empty except for the large chest the shadow people knocked over.

"I haven't seen the shadow people in a while," she told her parents.

"The house is better because we had a priest come," Frankie said. He pulled a stack of papers out from behind him. "This is on the 130-year history on this house. It includes everyone that's lived here." He handed it to Tyra. "And this is something we brought you from London." He handed her a box of cookies.

"Thank you," she said to him, hoping the shadow people would not come back and attack that night now that they were home. Tyra would lock herself in the room that night and read the house history and Abby's letters, or would that bring more ghosts?

• • • •

TYRA'S FOURTEENTH BIRTHDAY was in a few days. Her friends from school were coming, and she was worried about the ghosts.

"Maybe we can call the priest for another cleansing. I know they're here. I heard them," Margaret said, and Frankie agreed.

"We won't have my party at night, unless it drags on. They can all come in the early afternoon," Tyra said.

"I've ordered your birthday cake, and we'll have a lunch buffet instead of dinner. They all should be gone or going home by night," Margaret said.

"And we won't light candles. What will we do?" Tyra asked.

"Eat and open presents. We could have gold balloons and some music," Margaret thought out loud.

"I hope if they get bored, we won't have to entertain with ghosts. The Ouija board is gone. Hattie took it," Tyra pointed out. "I wonder if she'll ever come back?"

"It doesn't seem like it," Margaret said, unconfident.

As the hours went by, they didn't call the priest. They just thought of ways to entertain. Margaret had purchased the last of the gifts, and there were many.

"Do you think it's a good idea to have a birthday party at a haunted house?" Tyra asked.

"No. But if they figure it out, they might be entertained," Margaret answered.

"I'll tell Evelyn not to tell anyone. I hope the ghosts don't get angry they've been left out. I've got to go to school." Tyra hugged her parents and left abruptly.

• • • •

WHEN THE DAY OF THE party came, it was perfect. They had a lunch buffet prepared with a two-tier birthday cake, balloons, and gifts. Nobody knew the house was haunted. At lunch, Evelyn was the guest of honor, and Tyra sat at the end of the long dining table.

"Let's sing 'Happy Birthday,'" Margaret said.

Just as they all started the first note, the table began to shake, and tiny ghosts came flying out of the chandelier. A boy's mouth dropped in wonder. They flew to Tyra's hair, made it stand up, and flew into the dip, making it explode everywhere.

"Cool," Johnny from school said. Everyone stood up.

"I want to see more," Johnny said. He began walking around the house with his hands in his pockets. Other people followed.

They didn't find any ghosts, and so somebody's mother put her whole hand in the dip, feeling around for them.

Johnny tried the attic door, but Hattie had locked it before she left. "What's in here?" he asked.

"The attic. It's locked," Tyra answered.

"Is there any way we could get in?" he asked, and Abby let out a moan.

"My mom has the key," Tyra replied. There was a moment of silence, and people could be heard chatting downstairs loudly.

Margaret came up the stairs. "I think we'll call that priest again. They tried to wreck your party."

"Johnny wants to see the attic," Tyra said.

"Okay, but only for a little while." Margaret quickly got the large key ring out of her pocket and unlocked the attic door.

There was nothing to see but dusty old furniture and that chest. Cobwebs hung from the ceiling, and the sun was still shining brightly through the small window. The most interesting item was the chest. Johnny went straight to it and began looking.

"Those are her things," Tyra stated as Margaret watched.

"I'm going downstairs to clean up the dip." Margaret walked out the door and left it open.

"The ghost is Abby. She used to live here in the 1800s. I don't know how she died, but she's about our age. She and the shadow ghosts haunt us."

"Maybe she wants something," Johnny said.

"Maybe. It seems that way. There were boards the shadow ghosts pulled down outside. My dad must have removed them before the party. They hit someone."

"Why, though?" he asked.

"This place is a dump," Tyra said. "Where's Evelyn?"

"Probably trying not to eat the dip." They both laughed at Tyra's statement. "That's so Evelyn."

"Were you at the dance?" Johnny said, holding Abby's black-and-blue dress.

"I was, and I wore that." She pointed to the dress. "Let's go downstairs. The ghosts aren't coming."

As they walked down the stairs, he asked, "Do you want to go to the graduation dance with me?"

"Yes," she answered because he seemed nice.

"Great, I'll come get you."

As they predicted, Evelyn was at the table, staring at the dip. That late afternoon, some people left, but some had cake with a lot left over in the end. Ten people had attended the party. The gifts Tyra opened were great. She got a dress from Evelyn, a bracelet from Johnny, and scary books and games from her parents. They all cheered her up. Before he left, Johnny gave her a hug. The bracelet he got her was beautiful. It was the shiniest gold she had ever seen with a large rose—the perfect fashion accessory for 1929.

When Margaret sat down next to her, she asked, "How was it?"

"Perfect, but where's the puppy?" Tyra laughed.

"I guess we need one, huh?" Margaret laughed. "To scare away the ghosts."

"I can see him chasing a ghost. Can we?" Tyra held her hands like she was praying.

"I'll think about it," Margaret answered.

· · · ·

COME MORNING, MARGARET said they could get a puppy, but it might be a while. It was a comforting thought until Tyra got to school, and some kids were staring at her and whispering. Shortly after, Evelyn came her way.

"Word got out that you live in a haunted house. Kids are talking about coming and looking at your house," Evelyn said.

"Oh no! I don't want people looking in my windows." At the end of the day, it wasn't so bad, but Tyra couldn't wait to get back home.

Approaching home that warm afternoon, Tyra saw about twelve people standing outside—watching, waiting, and trying to see through the windows. She went in through the back door. A light flashed. Someone had taken a picture with a large camera. Tyra locked the door.

"Mom!" she called. "What is this?"

"I don't know. They've been out there. Someone at the party must have told the house is haunted." A knock sounded at the front door. Their first impression was to close the curtains and not answer the door, but the front curtains remained opened. Margaret opened the door.

"We've heard this house is haunted, and someone has even been injured. Is there any way we could come in?" a man asked.

"No." Margaret shook her head.

"What are you going to do about this?" he asked.

"We are calling a priest," she answered.

"That might work. We are interested in making this a haunted stop so people can see a haunted house, especially during October. Are you interested?" he asked.

"No, I don't think so" was all she could say.

"There's money in it for you." He handed her a business card. It said "The Haunted Attractions, Tim Terror."

Margaret rolled her eyes and tried not to laugh. "I'll talk to my husband, but I think we can work something out."

Tim smiled and looked in through the door.

The drapes were so beautiful. Some were red velvet, some sheer, and some off-white with a silky glow. "Come in." Margaret gestured for him to step through the door. He did, and Tyra went up to her room. They sat on the couch.

"I'm in."

"Great," he said and gave her a fifty-dollar advance.

She took it gladly. His name was great, but surely, his name wasn't really Terror.

Tim looked around. Margaret showed him the room they don't stay in anymore and told him about Tyra's ghost in the attic. "We can get this place ready in a month and start showing it off to people for money. You will get part of the profit."

Margaret nodded and called Tyra. "Tyra, get down here and tell this man about your ghost!"

Tyra came flying down. "Her name is Abby, and her stuff is in the attic. I don't know anything about her."

"I'll try to find out. If she died here or there's a mystery, people will want to know about it," he said.

"I was thinking about remodeling this summer," Margaret said.

"You can still do that! I'll see if my company can help you fund it. We can remodel this house to look like a creepy 1800s mansion," he said.

"That sounds great," Margaret said.

"Some places even allow you to spend the night in the haunted house. You can make more money, but we'll talk about that later," Tim added. "Can I look at all the rooms?" His assistant entered with a camera.

"Sure," Margaret said.

"We are going to put an article in the paper this week. Then, of course, when we're ready for people to walk through this house, there will be some kind of marketing in the newspaper again." With that, Tim headed for the second story; and just like a ghost hunter, he turned on his recorder to make notes and record anything out of the ordinary.

It sounded like a great plan, especially them covering the remodel. But Margaret had to think about what Frankie would say. Would he and Tyra want to live in a publicly haunted house? Before Tim left, he said he would be back in a week; and just as she had suspected, his name wasn't really Terror. It was just for entertainment.

Chapter Seven

The house was cleaned, and the heart of the house that used to be Margaret and Frankie's room was turned into a museum. Abby's dress and letters were on display with the letters in glass. Only one letter was open, and it talked about her time at camp. Other items from the chest were on display, and they dressed up the room to have an 1800s look by bringing down furniture from the attic and dusting them off. They still had a couple of pieces of wood that had been torn off the house by ghosts that were on display. They were considered cursed items.

When the priest that had come to bless the house heard what was happening, he was very troubled. He shook his head. "I don't know what went wrong when I tried to get rid of the ghosts. Sometimes the third time's the charm, and now they don't want me to come back to make it public. Maybe people will scare some of the ghosts away."

Tyra was not looking forward to strangers walking through her house. Frankie didn't feel like it was his house anymore, but they 100 percent owned it. Maybe it would be worth more once it was renovated, he hoped.

Tim Terror still didn't have Abby's story, and he had a feeling there was one. He decided to invent one until they found some juicy news or mystery about her. Could she still be missing? He wanted to write her story on a visitor's card with an illustration of her likeness and have people collect it as they left. The card was going to have only a summary of her fate.

Before people walked through, they were lucky to have a few knocks and footsteps from the attic. The strangers curiously walked around the house, mainly drawn to the upstairs and museum room. Tours started in the evening to make it seem creepier and more mysterious.

As the knocks and footsteps continued, they soon turned to banging. As Tyra listened in her room at night, she assumed the ghost was angry because her house was now a haunted house, and the shadow people were waiting to strike. If people were in danger, what was the point of having a haunted house? She tried to think of nicer things. Johnny would soon be taking her to the school dance, and then it would be summer shortly after. She and Evelyn were planning a lot of fun in the sun together.

Suddenly, a bright blue light flashed in Tyra's room. She got up and looked out her window. Another light flashed, and she spotted a few onlookers outside. Shaking her head in disgust, she closed the heavy curtains and opened her door. "Nuts!" she yelled.

Margaret came to the door. "What happened?"

"Someone took pictures of my window," Tyra replied.

"Get used to it. They're coming in a couple days to remodel the house," Margaret said. "It is going to look spooky."

Tyra quickly went downstairs and called Evelyn. "That's it. This is only half our home. There's a cursed object in my mother's old room. They are remodeling our house to look like a haunted mansion, and I don't even know if they found my real mother's body," she whined.

"Come over tomorrow, and we'll think of something. We have plenty of room," Evelyn said.

"Really?"

"Yes, we would love to have you. And who knows, maybe when the house is done, you'll like the new look," Evelyn said.

"Yes, but people will be staring at me when they walk through."

"Isn't that only during certain hours?" Evelyn asked.

"Oh, yeah, and at night. Thanks, Evelyn," Tyra said calmly.

"No problem. I'll ask my mom if you can stay with us while they're remodeling. They will be drilling, hammering, and making noise."

"Good idea."

Evelyn was quiet and had put down the phone to ask her mother. Suddenly, she said, "You can stay. We have to do chores, but you can stay the summer."

"Good. I'll ask my mother now."

Margaret seemed to like the idea, and they decided Tyra was to stay there for about a month.

"They are not remodeling the attic. A lot of the remodeling will be new walls. This house is so old it needs it. It will look sort of Victorian. They will be calling it the Shadows. I thought of the name for this house. Isn't it great? Tim is making a sign," Margaret said. "He's also busy creating Abby's story."

Her mother thought of a good name for the haunted house. But if it wasn't for Tyra, the ghost wouldn't be there. Tyra didn't say anything. She just lay down and thought about what she would pack for her stay with Evelyn.

"I don't like the idea of a haunted house here," Frankie said as he sat on the bed. "I don't like this room. It's too small for us."

"Let's just stay a while and make some money. I want to see how this house turns out, and they need to start haunted houses for Halloween. During that time, teenage boys play horrible tricks on the community. Last year, they messed with a dead body at the college," Margaret said.

"Okay, but I want to look at houses—newer houses," Frankie replied.

"At least now they are paying for renovations. All that money we saved for a remodel is now ours and can go toward a new house," Margaret said loudly.

"Yes, but I'm worried about how Tyra is taking all of this," Frankie said quietly.

"Tyra is leaving the day after tomorrow to stay with Evelyn. It is perfect." She hugged Frankie.

That was a good plan for her. Frankie agreed. Maybe it was a good idea to have the haunted house.

• • • •

EARLY IN THE DAY, TIM Terror came and was eager to ask Margaret how everything was going. He was pleased to find it was just fine. "I do have Abby's story here printed on each one of these cards. Can I place it in the museum room?"

Margaret nodded in agreement, and he stepped in. "This is what I have, a summary of her short tragic life here."

Abby's Story

In the year 1890, Abigail lived here at 15 Cedars Lane. She was a fourteen-year-old girl just like the others and had just returned from camp. That night, while unpacking her clothes she took to that camp, she found a beaded necklace she had made there. While walking through the second-floor hallway, she tried to slide it over her head. But in the effort, it got stuck and broke. The large beads fell everywhere, and some rolled to the stairs. It was a new moon that night and especially dark. When she walked to the stairs, she slipped and fell down the stairs headfirst. When her parents found her at the bottom, she was dead. Her neck was broken.

Her parents were so saddened they moved to another town and had a baby boy. When there's a full moon, the ghost haunts the house, especially the staircase, looking for the beads and her parents.

"You created this?" Margaret asked.

"No, it's true. People say they saw her on a full moon, even looking through the windows. Some people think she may get her power from the moon. Or because she died in a dark house when there was no moon, she is now angry and wants to haunt when the moon is out, and during a full moon, there is more light." Tim went to place the cards at Abby's display. "Is the attic locked?"

"No," Margaret answered.

"You should probably lock it so curious customers don't wander up there and steal." Tim began walking to the attic.

"We all think the ghost lives there," Margaret said.

He opened the attic door a little. "She must have been up there quite a while, and Tyra conjured her up."

Margaret shut the door and locked it. "My husband's right—it is getting hard to live here. There are three of us in the second story, and the rooms are small. One of them is haunted, and the attic stairs are by our rooms. Frankie wants to move when the house is done being renovated, and Tyra is staying with Evelyn soon."

"Tyra will be gone? That's not a bad idea. We can work day and night. In the end, the haunted house is ours. But we would buy it from you, of course," Tim said.

"That's great. We would have to talk to my husband, of course. How long will renovations take?" she asked.

"About a month," he said. "I have a sign in my car that says 'The Shadows.' We may put it up before renovations are done." With that, Tim went to his car.

That day, Tyra went to school, then came home to pack. Late that night, the moon shone through her window. Suddenly, Tyra heard moaning and sobbing.

Abby appeared, crying. "Why do you have to go?"

"Have you noticed? This is a haunted house now," Tyra said.

"Of course." The ghost rolled her eyes. "I want you to stay. We can live together, but I want to haunt the customers. I hate them and their curiosity!"

"It's not their fault you're dead. I have to go, but I'll be back in a month," Tyra reassured.

"I'll be around when the moon is full. Where are you going?" Abby had stopped crying.

"Evelyn's." Tyra sounded tired.

"Oh, I might know where that is. I want to come visit you a few times a month or more," the ghost suggested.

"Okay, just keep it quiet," Tyra said.

"Goodbye, Tyra. Until the next moon," Abigail said.

"Goodbye, Abby."

"Can I be your other best friend?" Abby asked.

"Sure, I can have two: one living and one dead." They both giggled.

The ghost walked straight through the shut door.

Tyra was wide awake and staring at the ceiling before surrendering to sleep.

Chapter Eight

Evelyn and her mother, Susan, came to pick up Tyra to stay with them. Susan wore a bun in her hair on that warm day. There was hardly a breeze.

Tyra had only one suitcase, and as they rode to Evelyn's house, they passed the cemetery and Nathaniel's old house. It looked like it was condemned. No one would live there anymore. There was a large mound on her mother's grave. She was once again sound asleep in her grave.

When they left the city and drove on a road with nothing around, Tyra knew they were close to Evelyn's. She had been there only two times before, and it was nice. Suddenly, there it was, with many trees on both sides. It seemed as peaceful as ever. It was a large house like Tyra's, but much newer. Her house was built in the late 1700s, but this one was built in the late 1800s. The roof was dark blue, which added a nice touch. Geese ran nearby and flew to the lake almost a mile away.

Evelyn and her mother got out of the car. It was a four-bedroom house, and three people lived there. "Do you want to stay with me or in your own room?" Evelyn asked. They had two extra.

"I would like to stay in my own room," Tyra answered.

They went upstairs. There were two guest rooms, and Tyra picked the one closest to Evelyn's. Her parents stayed downstairs. "I'll stay by you."

"Perfect." They went in the room and sat down.

"Have you ever seen a ghost in your house?" Tyra asked.

"No," Evelyn replied.

"Let's be sisters," Tyra said.

"Okay, good idea. Want to celebrate with s'mores? We can make them on the oven."

"Okay," Tyra said, and they both went downstairs to make them.

Evelyn showed her how to use the oven.

The s'mores were good, but they wanted lunch. "Let's make soup over the oven," Evelyn said. When they did, Tyra showed she could use the oven, and it was easy for her to use.

Tyra could see the pantry, and it was stocked with a lot of items to cook with.

Evelyn's mother entered and opened a window in the stuffy house. "Tonight, we're having chicken and rice for dinner."

"Oh, good! Do you like chicken and rice, Ty?" asked Evelyn.

"Yes," she responded. Tyra went to the window and looked out. It was different from where she lived, and she would have to get used to the quiet with no other houses, but she liked it.

"Tyra, I want to show you the lake. Mom, can you drive us?"

"Yes, in a little bit. We'll go, and then I'll have to stop by the market and get some chicken," her mother answered.

"Ty, later on, let's fix up the other bedroom like a small family room. We'll turn the daybed into a couch and load the bookcase with more books and games. Mom, can we take your radio up there?" Evelyn asked.

"Yes, of course. That sounds like a good idea. I'll bring up some pillows as well. When we're out, we can get you guys more books and games. And at the store, we'll get some more food you and Tyra like. But I don't want you guys to leave that room a mess, and straighten up your rooms every day, okay?"

"Okay," both girls answered.

Both girls really liked the lake, and they decided they would go back later that week to lie in the sun. As they looked at the lake, the geese honked, and a turtle jumped in the water with a splash. This was so much better than the Shadows.

They walked from store to store. Tyra's first day with Evelyn and her mom was busy and tiring. They bought so much each one of them had to carry a bag. When they got home, they passed out, hungry.

As Tyra lay next to Evelyn, she whispered, "I saw my mom's grave when we were driving by the cemetery. It looked okay, but freshly dug."

"It's back the way it was," Evelyn answered. "Dinner should be soon."

After dinner, they began putting together the mini family room, and Evelyn's mother helped. When everything was brought up, Susan brought up a small plant to put on top of the bookcase.

"Wow!" Evelyn said with a giggle.

"I want to sleep up here. Do you want to sleep up here?" Tyra asked.

"Yes." Evelyn began grabbing pillows and blankets for them to sleep on. One girl on the floor and one on the bed.

Tyra thought dinner was delicious, and when the day was over, they went to the family room and shut the door. It was deathly quiet. "We should sleep here every night," Tyra suggested.

"Yes," Evelyn answered.

"Really, I want to sleep here all week," Tyra said.

They did sleep there all week and made many attempts to clean the rooms. The week was filled with games, sun, and radio shows. At the end, Tyra wanted to call her mother, and Evelyn let her use the phone.

"You should," Evelyn said.

Tyra agreed and began calling home. She gave all positive comments about her stay at Evelyn's, and Margaret confirmed they had started remodeling.

"The house will look scary when it's done, won't it?" Tyra asked on the phone, unsure.

"Yes, but don't worry. Your father is looking for another house," Margaret responded.

"Was it really loud?" Tyra asked.

"Yes, and it will be even louder tomorrow." Margaret's line sounded staticky.

"I'll bet Abby's pissed. Lock your door tonight," Tyra said cautiously.

"I will, monster," Margaret said, trying to sound loving.

"I'll call you in a week," Tyra said and then hung up the phone.

That night, she lay there, wondering what was happening at the Shadows.

Chapter Nine

As Tyra sat on the living room couch, the house began creaking, and there was scratching near the back door. "Did you hear that?" she called to Evelyn.

"Yes, let's see if it stops," Evelyn answered.

As the sky darkened, the noises kept coming, slowly, then faster. When Tyra looked out the window, she saw wind blowing a tree, making it scratch the wall. "Do you have rats?"

"I don't know. I'll ask my mom to set traps. Are you wondering if it's ghosts?" Evelyn asked.

"Yes. I am not sure if the shadow people have followed me." Tyra wasn't sure about them, but she knew Abby would follow her. She gave her permission to, and she was sure Abby asked so she could freely come and go. That was a secret she would not tell Evelyn.

"Let's make a dowsing rod and pendulum. We can ask it if ghosts are here making those sounds." Evelyn grabbed wire from the storage room and what used to be a necklace with a large crystal on the end. She twisted the wire like a boomerang and put the pendulum in her pocket. "Show me exactly where those noises came from," she said to Tyra.

"The backyard tree made some of them, but the rest came from there." Tyra pointed to the back door.

They listened to the wall. "I don't hear anything now," Evelyn said. She held the dowsing rod to the wall. "Is there anything here?" she asked. The rod jerked down.

"What did that?" Tyra asked.

"The wind probably." Evelyn took out her pendulum and held it over the counter.

Tyra did not believe the wind could have moved that rod.

They stood there as the pendulum began to twirl. "Are there ghosts here?" The pendulum stopped, and they knew it was a "no."

More sounds came, but now it sounded like digging and long nails skittering across the floor. It was an animal. "I'll tell my mother. Maybe it's a possum."

Tyra nodded and grabbed the pendulum. "Let me try." As Tyra held it, the pendulum swung wildly. "Are the ghosts coming?" It swung so hard she let go, and it flew from her fingers and landed in the living room.

"That's not good," Evelyn said. "I'll try to think of something to keep the ghosts out."

Tyra's eye got large, and she didn't move. She knew Abby was coming.

"What? What is this about?" Evelyn grabbed Tyra. "What do you know?"

"I don't know anything." Tyra stepped back.

"Are you sure the ghosts aren't coming? Did they threaten you?" Evelyn asked.

"No, they didn't threaten me. But I've been afraid they'd come ever since I got here."

"I suppose there's nothing we can do anyways. There's nowhere we could go. Let's try to go to bed. We have to help my mother make about fifty cupcakes for the fair tomorrow," Evelyn said, and she grabbed the rod and pendulum and put them in a drawer.

As they walked upstairs, Evelyn said, "We will make the cupcakes tomorrow, then sell them at the fair the following day."

"In a few days, I'd like to call my mother," Tyra said. "The fair ought to be fun."

"Oh yes! You can do whatever you want while we sell the cupcakes. I hope you brought plenty of money," Evelyn said.

"Yes, my mother gave me some," Tyra responded. She had heard of the fair. It was big and would make her stay there worthwhile.

• • • •

IN THE MORNING, THE wind had blown the trees so hard there were green leaves and small branches everywhere. Evelyn began picking them up. As Susan watched from the kitchen window, she said, "My mother said she would set a trap today. She wants to start mixing the cupcake batter soon. There will be vanilla, strawberry, and chocolate cupcakes. Sounds good, and they'll go for like five cents."

Tyra nodded and began picking up leaves, which they put in a box to help clean up. As she walked to the back door, she could see white chips of paint from the wall on the ground. She pointed to them. "See," she said to Evelyn.

"Oh my gosh, there's a werewolf out here!" Evelyn joked.

"It's not funny," Tyra said.

"What could have done this?" Evelyn asked.

"Anything," Tyra responded.

Susan motioned for them to come in.

"What are we going to do to help your mother?" asked Tyra.

Evelyn opened the back door and went in. There were three mixing bowls there.

"Each one of us will mix one large bowl of batter. That will make enough cupcakes for around fifty people. One will be vanilla. Tyra can mix chocolate. And you, Evelyn, can mix strawberry," Susan said.

They each got a little apron and mixed all the contents with Evelyn's mother.

Watching what they were doing, Susan nodded in approval. "You have to mix it fast," she told them.

"I wonder what's happening at the Shadows," Tyra said to Evelyn as she mixed the batter with a large spoon.

"Your mother will tell you in a few days," Evelyn said.

"Yes, she's great," Tyra said.

Susan went to grab frosting buckets from the pantry.

"What about the Shadows?" Evelyn asked.

"They understand my feelings about the haunted house. We are moving," Tyra answered.

"That's great."

"What?" Evelyn's mother came out and put three different-flavored buckets on the table.

"Tyra's moving. She doesn't want to live in a haunted house. I can't blame her," Evelyn said.

"Really?" said Susan.

"Yes. They are renovating it and turning it into a haunted attraction, especially for Halloween. It doesn't seem like a real home anymore," Tyra replied.

"That's too bad," Susan said. Then she got cups ready to pour the different batters into. The oven wasn't large, so they couldn't cook them all at once. "Looks good, girls," she said, then poured her batter into the cups and shoved them into the oven for a demonstration.

They covered their bowls until it was time to bake them. It took hours, and they had more than fifty cupcakes. The fair was going to be perfect, and Tyra couldn't wait to tell her mother.

The following day at the fair, Tyra wore her hair up and a white flower-print dress with lace trim. Susan and Evelyn wore Sunday dresses. The cupcakes were lined up on a table separated by flavors like a rainbow. People flocked to their table, and at lunchtime, the three ladies closed their table and had lunch.

After po'boy sandwiches, which were Tyra's favorite, they wanted to have fun. Tyra won a few stuffed animals, and when they got back to their table, most of the cupcakes were gone. When they sold a few more, it was time to go home. Susan was tired, and the girls wanted to go.

"Don't eat the rest of the cupcakes until after dinner," Susan said.

Evelyn went up to her room to nap before dinner.

Tyra asked, "Can I call my mother? I really want to talk to her."

"Sure," Susan answered and then went to prepare dinner.

Tyra told her mother how the fair was a good experience as she sat at the kitchen table. "Have you heard anything from the ghosts?"

"Just some footsteps. Tim put a sign in front of the house that says 'The Shadows.' Nobody is walking through it right now. They are knocking down the wall that separates your room from the one next to it so the room will be bigger. Frankie wants a bigger room so we want to stay in it, and you can stay in the room at the end of the hall that used to be Hattie's room. She wants to come back. Do you need her to help you with anything?" Margaret asked.

"I can always use help decorating, and I don't mind switching rooms. It will be a good change." Tyra knew she wouldn't have to stay as close to her parents anymore. That was a good idea to her. "Do you know when we are moving?"

"No. But hopefully, this summer. Your father hasn't found a house yet," Margaret answered.

"I miss Hattie, and I'm glad the haunted room downstairs was turned into a mini museum. Hattie got hurt in there. Is the priest coming?" Tyra asked.

"No, I don't think so."

"He could bless the museum room, and that will mean it's safe, and it won't scare off the ghosts upstairs. Abby won't ever leave," Tyra said.

"That's a good idea, Ty," Margaret answered. "People aren't outside taking pictures anymore. We were in the newspaper a little while ago. It's been so quiet."

"Mom, you don't know where she is?" Tyra kept her voice low. Susan was in the kitchen, cooking.

"Abby?"

"Yes, she's probably wandering around 'cause I'm not there," Tyra said.

"That's what we thought," Margaret added.

"We thought the ghosts may have followed me here, but the pendulum indicated no. Maybe they didn't get in. Maybe it's just not a full moon. She needs that, Mom."

"Yes, so I've read. Call me if anything out of the ordinary happens, Ty."

"How is the house coming along?" Tyra asked.

"It's almost half done. It's pretty big, but they went for the walls first," Margaret said.

"The next full moon is in a couple of weeks. I'll be waiting for Abby."

Susan kept stirring her sauce, minding her own business.

"I miss the Shadows. Me and Evelyn will be out. Can we stop by and visit you?" Tyra asked.

"Of course you can," Margaret answered, glad to hear it. Her daughter had grown so much lately, and she wanted to see her being responsible and visiting her mother. She was busy cleaning after the remodelers and moving into the bigger bedroom.

"I can't wait to see the house. I can help move my things into Hattie's old room. Do you think you will like the house better?" Tyra asked.

"Yes, especially with the bigger room," Margaret responded.

"Okay, I'd better go. It's dinnertime. We'll be by tomorrow." Tyra hung up after her mother said goodbye. She couldn't wait. Things were really working out.

When Evelyn and Tyra stopped by their house, Margaret was so glad to see them. "You're here! They've gotten a lot of work done these last two weeks." She hugged Tyra.

All the girls wanted to do was see the house. "This is different. Everything's so new." To Tyra, it didn't look very Victorian. She went to her old bedroom. "It's much bigger." She began dragging her belongings out.

"Just put it in the hallway toward the other room. We'll arrange everything, and we can use the museum room's walk-in closet as a storage room. All of our furniture will go into your renovated old room."

As Tyra moved everything out, Evelyn and Margaret began dragging the bedframe up the stairs. They all helped with the large mattress.

After an hour, Tyra had put all her things into Hattie's old room. All that was left was her bed, which was put downstairs in the museum room.

When Margaret was done fixing the new room she would share with Frankie, she put a small brown vase with a daisy in it for the finishing touches. "There, maybe this could be a house again. It doesn't look so scary anymore."

"Wouldn't it have been creepier if they didn't remodel and left it old-looking?" Tyra asked.

"Yes, but I think Tim wanted to help. Do you want to stay now?" Margaret asked.

Tyra hesitated. "I miss this room. Abby would walk above me to let me know she's mad. I guess that's over. Hattie's room is more peaceful." She did not want to mention Abby would stop in her room so her mother wouldn't freak. "Did Dad find a house?"

"He has a few houses he's interested in. We'll see. He'll have to take me by to see them," Margaret said.

"So when do you think they'll finish this house?" Tyra asked as they walked down the stairs.

"In a couple of weeks," her mom answered.

"We have to go to the market now for Evelyn's mom. I'll see ya." Tyra and Evelyn left and began walking straight to the store.

"We can be blood sisters. Do you want to?" Tyra asked.

"Yes." Evelyn nodded.

"If you have something sharp, we sterilize it, cut ourselves, and join those cuts. That way, we are blood sisters. Tonight," Tyra said.

"We can use my mother's really sharp needle she uses when she sews. She always cuts herself," Evelyn said.

That night, after Susan went to bed, the girls were ready to become blood sisters. Evelyn had already swiped the needle from her mom's room. They both pricked themselves near their nails, and blood came. They joined their fingers together and held them there.

"Now we'll always be sisters," Tyra said.

As they stood there, becoming sisters, the blood began to drip a little. As seconds went by, there was more, and they heard a door creak. They separated their fingers. "It's your mom," Tyra said.

Evelyn grabbed paper towels for them, and they heard footsteps. When the person appeared, they saw it wasn't Susan, but the ghost Abby.

"Abby!" Tyra said.

"Can I do it too?" she asked.

"You don't have any blood," Tyra said.

Abby came closer. "It's not a full moon, but I thought I'd come."

They looked at Evelyn. "It's okay with me. I've never hung out with a ghost before."

"You're early, before the full moon, but it's okay," Tyra said. "Did you make all that blood run?"

"Yes. Sorry, I didn't mean to. You know it may be because I did not get power from the full moon yet. See, I'm dimmer." Abby held out her arms, and she did indeed look a little dimmer. She lit up a little with white in her dress and light blue around the edges. They all sat on the floor.

Abby looked around, afraid. "Evelyn, is your father here?"

"Yes, he just works a lot."

Tyra thought Abby's colors were pretty. "What's your last name, Abby? Tim never told us."

"Anthony, Abigail Anthony," she answered.

"That's beautiful," both girls agreed.

"Next week is my last week here."

"I wish you would come home," Abby said.

"The house isn't done. I'd have to ask my mother. I can ask her tomorrow," Tyra said.

Just then, Abby began fading. "I'm going. I'm out of power. I hope you come." Abby flew out the window and faded away. The moon was still waxing.

• • • •

IN THE MORNING, MARGARET said Tyra could come home, but not for a few days. But the house was almost done. Tyra was ready to go, and she packed. The next few days were spent in the family room, and the girls played games and listened to the radio.

Chapter Eleven

The renovators didn't have much left to do but replace the wood on the outside and clean up. They were also going to repaint the outside of the house white. That day, the house looked newer again, and Tyra wanted to go home and see what it was like sleeping in Hattie's old room.

That night, she went quietly out to the kitchen, opened a drawer, and took out the pendulum and dowsing rod. She went up to her room and put them under her clothes in the suitcase.

The following morning, Margaret came to pick her up. Before going out the door, Tyra said to Evelyn, "Thanks for letting me stay. I'll see you in school. Bye." She waved to Susan and went out the door, carrying her suitcase and a bag with her stuffed animals from the fair.

She was so glad to be home. Evelyn's was becoming boring to her anyway. She stopped in the living room, listening for ghosts. She didn't hear any.

"Hattie might be coming by sometime this week. She's not in school right now and wants to see us again," Margaret said.

"I won't need help with homework until September," Tyra said.

And then her mother said it: "Frankie found a house. I still have to see it, but he said it's perfect and within our budget.

All Tyra could say was "I like the sign out front. I need to go upstairs and start arranging my room so it's mine now and not the guest room Hattie stayed in."

"Let's both go look at this house. Maybe you will like it. I'll let you pick your room. And, Tyra, it's Victorian," Margaret said to make Tyra feel better.

Tyra stood at the top of the stairs and said, "Sounds great."

Then she walked down the hall and went to her new room with her belongings and dropped them near the closet. She unpacked and put the divination tools in the dresser. After lying on the bed, Tyra twisted and turned, knowing she could never get comfortable until she had her old bed.

After setting up the bed with her old sheets and gray blanket and eating dinner, Tyra was lying on her bed when she heard it—shuffling sounds coming from the attic. It didn't sound like Abby, but the full moon was coming soon. She walked down the hall to the attic stairs. "Hello?"

There was a strange male laugh, and she assumed it was the shadow people. They were still there. She tried to turn the attic doorknob, but it was locked. She whispered, "Is this the shadow people?"

A small voice answered, "Yes."

Tyra ran to her room and locked the door. It was pitch-dark, so she opened the curtains a little for some waxing moonlight. The house was practically still the same and didn't look Victorian. The next house probably wouldn't either. She didn't want to move.

When the morning light woke Tyra, she walked to the stairs and found Hattie.

Hattie pointed to the grand piano by the stairs. "Something or an animal was scratching the wall last night."

They closely inspected the small scratches on the wall—small scratches that could have been made by a small shadow person.

"Last night, I heard them in the attic. It must have been them, and they sounded small. I heard them speak," Tyra said.

"Can I spend the night tonight to investigate the sounds? I want to see what happens," Hattie asked Margaret.

"Yes, but where will you sleep?" Margaret asked.

"On the small couch downstairs in the storage room," Hattie answered. It looked more like a sewing room but had a door and seemed safe, though it was near the museum room.

"Okay, sounds good," Margaret said. "That's a good idea because Frankie and I are going out tonight, and I don't want Tyra alone."

"Perfect! The ghost may try to haunt," Hattie said to herself. "When are more people coming to see the haunted house?"

"I don't know," Margaret replied. "No one's coming, and we're moving. They will want it open on Halloween. I should ask Tim."

"We don't want any surprises," Hattie said.

"I'll call Tim now and make sure no one's coming tonight. Also, Tyra is too old for a babysitter, but she will think I called you to come because we'll be gone. If she asks you, just tell her you wanted to investigate and I don't want you alone," Margaret said.

"Okay, that's a good idea. Where's the key to the attic?" Hattie asked.

"It's in the kitchen cabinet," Margaret answered. "You don't need to go in there, and I don't want Tyra in there. We took the antique furniture out and put it in the museum room anyway, the chest as well, and Abigail's dress is on display."

Hattie nodded and went to the museum room to take a look. It looked like a room from the 1800s. The furniture was dusted and perfectly placed. Abby's dress stood clean and tall. Hattie noticed the bottom of the dress had black strings hanging and looked like it was coming apart, possibly because they had the dress cleaned. That dress was way too old for Tyra to wear. The whole room was a trip back in time, though the four-poster bed wasn't a real antique.

Hattie crashed on it and stared straight up. As she did, she noticed a green-and-yellow Tiffany lamp next to the bed. Margaret stepped in, and Hattie said, "You should wallpaper this place with old-fashioned wallpaper."

"It's nice," Margaret said.

"Yes, until you read the sign outside that says 'The Shadows.' It will remind people that this house is a shadow of the past—a tragedy that happened to the Anthonys."

As Hattie stepped into the sewing room, she was ready to stay there. But it was another small room, and the museum room was tempting to hang out in.

When late afternoon came, Margaret came to announce that she and Frankie wanted to go see a play, then have dinner at a restaurant. The girls were to eat what was prepared in the fridge.

"What do you think your mom will do about those scratches?" Hattie asked Tyra when Margaret left.

"Nothing. I think Abby is coming back, and you're staying right next to her memory," Tyra said.

"Do you think your mom will let me stay here a few days?" Hattie asked.

"Yes."

"When is the next full moon?" Hattie asked.

"Tonight. Just kidding. Soon, probably in the next few days. Chicken?" Tyra asked.

"No. Because you're Terra's daughter, does that mean you're not scared of anything?"

"Yes, but it's not true," she whispered.

"Why are you whispering?" Hattie asked.

"Because the ghost can listen, and we won't know it."

Tyra got up to leave the room, but Hattie stopped her.

"Do you want me to stay downstairs with you tonight?" Tyra asked concerned.

"Yes. Where will you stay?"

"On the floor in here. Why does it seem so safe in here?" Tyra asked.

"Because we are together. We are not supposed to go into the attic," Hattie said.

Tyra nodded. "How smart of Margaret. The ghosts live there. We should never go in there again. When we move, you will be coming to our new house to see us, and it won't be called the Shadows. It will be the perfect house in the forest, I'm guessing, since that's what Frankie has probably found."

They both made beds on the sewing room floor. They heard plenty of noises, but they sounded like they were coming from outside. Then came the loudest of all—a ghost was banging a song on the grand piano, and for a little while, scratching could be heard like the song was being played around the sound. They shut the bedroom door and locked it.

"I wish I had something to investigate, but that's definitely a ghost," Hattie said.

Footsteps could be heard in the room next to them—Abby's. There wasn't a window in that room, and they couldn't see the moon, but they had a small light.

They stayed in the room for an hour, and the noises stopped. Tyra slowly opened the door and ran to the piano. Her mother was coming home soon.

Chapter Twelve

Tyra and Margaret had both gone to look at the new house Frankie had found. It was clean, and the rooms were bigger. Tyra picked a room that was large compared to her old room, and it had pink walls and a wooden floor.

They all wanted to move. They just didn't want the ghosts to follow them. Margaret was already talking about the rugs she wanted to purchase and lay on the wooden floor. It was peaceful out there and closer to Evelyn's house and Tyra's school.

The deal was made, and the house was bought. "There," Frankie said after he paid the owner. "I think we'll keep the furniture we need like beds and sell the rest."

"Yes, except I have two groups of people that want to see our haunted house. After that, it's Tim Terror's business," Margaret said.

"That's true. I want to get in here ASAP. As you know, Tim Terror has already bought our old house," he said.

"I wonder what he'll do with it," Margaret wondered aloud, and they laughed.

Frankie and Margaret spent the next few days packing and taking what they wanted to the new house. Frankie did manage to sell a few pieces of furniture but left the rest for Tim's haunted house business.

"Yes, these scratches on the wall are perfect. How did you make those?" Tim asked, rubbing the scratches that were near the piano.

"I didn't. I hear small shadow people did that themselves—ghosts that I have sold to you with this house," Frankie pointed out.

"The scratches are perfect," Tim said.

• • • •

THE SMYTHES' FIRST day in their house was great. There was not a single peep except from the trees outside.

Tim sat in his haunted house by himself, holding the keys to it. He was trying to come up with a new haunted house idea. He couldn't decide how to make anything seem real. The house was mostly empty except for the museum room. There were things to think about, like if he wanted to furnish it or keep all that room and make a fake haunted house. But the real ghosts would help too.

As he wandered around the house, Tim began to hear a scratching noise. He ran to the scratches by the stairs but couldn't tell where the noise was coming from. The scratches got louder and wouldn't stop.

"Would you stop that!" he yelled, but they just kept coming. Tim's heart beat fast, and he ran upstairs to the attic. It was so dark and dusty that night. Light from the full moon shone through the attic window and lit up the webs. He kicked up dust as he ran downstairs.

The scratches sounded deeper in the wall, like something was coming through. He glanced out the downstairs window and saw nothing but his sign for the haunted house. "Help!" Tim yelled as he ran to the museum room and shut the door.

As he looked at Abby's display, she appeared behind him. She was pale and strong as ever. She lifted a blade and destroyed him from the inside. He let out a final scream.

"No more haunted house," Abby sarcastically said in an echoing voice, ending his business. She now had the house to herself.

• • • •

"IT'S TERRIBLE WHAT happened to Tim Terror," Margaret said, peeling vegetables in her new kitchen. She was planning to plant her own vegetable garden. "The police don't know who did it, but I think it was those ghosts. We have to do something."

"The Shadows is now closed. It's a crime scene. We will call the priest and try to get rid of the ghosts again. That house now belongs to Tim's haunting company. It's worth a shot. Abby must be destroyed, and if we do get rid of those ghosts, we won't have to worry about them following Tyra here," Frankie said.

The priest did another blessing on the house. It was quiet, and Tim's haunting company wanted to let people walk through it more to make money. After the murder, there was a huge turnout of people. The house was in demand, and they could not keep it closed. Nobody saw a shadow ghost again, but they reported hearing Abby's footsteps upstairs as they walked through. And just as Tim had thought, they loved to see the scratch marks a ghost had made on the wall. Tim's murder was a part of the attraction like Abby, and he had become a legend in his own haunted attraction.

Just as she wanted, Abby moved freely around the house, haunting the stairs. It was her favorite place to be. All the attention made her want to leave the house for a while and even find Tyra to be with her again.

Chapter Thirteen

On an August night, Tyra daydreamed about starting high school. She planned to go back to school shopping with her mother. Sitting on the floor, she glanced at the moonlight outside the window, and Abby's face appeared. Tyra shut the curtains, knowing she was back. Would she ever get away from this ghost?

Tyra went downstairs, making sure all the doors and windows were locked.

"What are you doing?" Margaret asked.

"Abby, I saw Abby," Tyra said.

"How did she find you?"

"Don't get upset. Before I went to stay with Evelyn, I told Abby she could visit me there. She probably asked so that she could keep coming," Tyra explained.

"Okay. Don't do that again. And if you can, tell her she can't stay with you," Margaret said.

"I don't know if that will work, but I will try," Tyra said.

When Tyra left the room, Margaret herself began praying to bless the house and then placed wooden rosary beads in the table drawer in the living room.

When Frankie came home, she asked him to do it as well.

"Tyra said she saw Abby. We should keep her away from her and our home. It's the only plan I can come up with. I will ask the company that Tim worked for to make sure to keep the Shadows open. That will make Abby want to haunt the customers, and she'll maybe stay away from this house," Margaret said.

"That sounds like a good idea," Frankie replied.

"I don't know if Tyra can ask Abby not to come back," Margaret said. "She hasn't exactly seen her in the house yet, but she was outside."

It was a good plan until one night shortly after, during the waning moon, customers were walking up the old haunted house's stairs when

Abby appeared and pushed a young man down the stairs. He was killed in seconds. His friends ran in shock. The Shadows was officially over, but Abby remained. She had gotten her revenge.

Tyra was afraid to speak to Abby, and she kept quiet. The only option was to condemn the haunted house, and as Abby watched from the stairs, men hammered boards over the doors and windows. 'The Shadows' sign fell to the left a little when someone threw a rock at it.

"Didn't they know this place was dangerous?" the man asked.

"Yes, they wanted to make money," his companion answered and threw a rock, and they drove away.

Tyra went on seeing Johnny, and they started high school. It was going smoothly. When her parents brought home a newspaper, there was a small article about Nathaniel Johnston. Tyra really wanted to know what happened to her father. It explained a man was arrested for his murder, but they still needed to prove to a judge that he was guilty.

The man swore up and down he was innocent until they found his prints on the axe. He was given life and moved to a prison in Chicago. People heard him say he was glad to spend his time behind bars because it would keep him safe from ghosts. But some nights, he could hear ghostly banging, chopping, and wailing on a full moon night.

Did you love *Tyra of the Shadows*? Then you should read *The Haunted Rosebuds*[1] by Martha Wickham!

Lana is a psychic ghost hunter working in The Circle Of Roses shop. She wants to help solve a case when a man's wife leaves him because of ghosts tormenting her in the attic, but she ends up with a haunting dilemma of her own. Terra's ghost is haunting one of her teens in her small townhouse.Sylvie and Dana are teenagers who just want to live but when Sylvie's room is repeatedly thrashed, psychic Rose is called to investigate. She knows Terra from way back and thinks she wants more revenge, but why is the other teen Dana not affected? Sylvie and Dana have their own group called the Rosebuds. Started when they were kids, they wind up the only two in it. When old enough they will go into training to become real psychics. As for this story it is their first

---

1. https://books2read.com/u/bOpJ2g

2. https://books2read.com/u/bOpJ2g

everything, except their first time seeing a ghost. How long can Terra's ghost be kept a secret from Dana? And will Rose be able to solve both cases at once?

Read more at https://readmarthawickham.com/.

About the Author

Martha has studied writing with Writer's Digest and has an associate's degree. She has also written poems and songs and has even studied screen writing and horror at one time. She still practices writing and likes getting writing prompts, and her favorite author is VC Andrews. Listen to her hot new audiobooks at your favorite retailer.

Read more at https://readmarthawickham.com/.